BERNARD WANTS A BABY

BERNARD WANTS A BABY

To Brooke

BY

JOAN ELIZABETH GOODMAN

ILLUSTRATED BY

DOMINIC CATALANO

Best,

For Henry, who wanted a baby brother, and for Juliet, who got one
—J. E. G.

For Alex
—D. C.

BERNARD WANTS A BABY. Text copyright © 2004 by
Joan Elizabeth Goodman, illustrations copyright © 2004
by Dominic Catalano. Reprinted by Zaner-Bloser, Inc. for
its Voices program by arrangement with Boyds Mills Press.
Publisher Cataloging-in-Publication Data (U.S.)
Goodman, Joan E.
Bernard wants a baby / by Joan Elizabeth Goodman ;
illustrated by Dominic Catalono.—1st ed.
(32) p : col. ill. ; cm.
Summary: Bernard the young elephant hopes for a baby
brother and gets more than he wished for.
ISBN 1-59078-088-4
1. Brothers and sisters — Fiction. 2. Babies — Fiction.
3. Elephants — Fiction. I. Catalano, Dominic, ill. II. Title
[E] 21 PZ7.G61375Ber 2004
2003108228

ISBN: 978-07367-9302-5

Zaner-Bloser, Inc., P.O. Box 16764, Columbus, Ohio
43216-6764

1-800-421-3018

www.zaner-bloser.com

Printed in China   11 12 13 14 15 (22515) 5 4 3 2 1

Bernard wanted a baby more than anything in the world.
"I want a baby," said Bernard.
"We'll just have to wait and see," said Grandma.

"I don't want that
spit-up kind of baby,"
Bernard told Grandma
when they went to the park.

6

7

"I don't want a sister kind of baby," Bernard said to Papa when they were shopping.

"Sisters can be nice," said Papa.

"No sisters," said Bernard. "I want a brother named Max."

One night at bedtime Bernard told Mama, "I really don't want a crying baby."

Mama patted her tummy. "Sometimes babies cry."

"Not my Max," said Bernard. He yawned and went to sleep.

The very next day, Mama went to the hospital to have the baby. Papa went with her. Grandma and Bernard had to stay at home.

"It's not fair," said Bernard.

Papa came home that night.

"Where's Mama?" asked Bernard.

"She's resting," said Papa. "Tomorrow, I'll bring her home with your brand new—"

"My very own baby brother!" shouted Bernard.

"Yes," said Papa. "And there are two surprises!"

"Two presents?" asked Bernard.

"You'll see," said Papa.

Bernard dreamed that baby Max
gave him two great big presents.

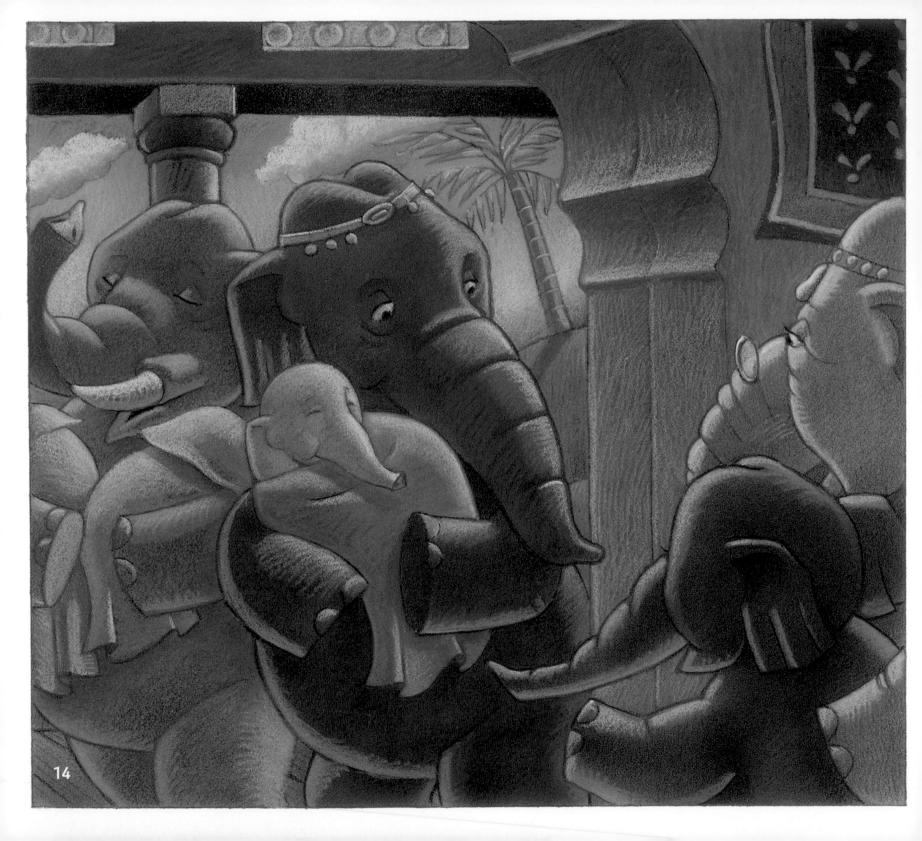

Mama came home, carrying Baby Max all wrapped up in blankets.

"I want to hold him," said Bernard.

"Come sit with me. You can hold Max, and Papa will show you the surprises," said Mama.

Bernard held Max very carefully. Max yawned and smiled. He was a perfect little baby.

Papa sat next to Bernard, holding two more bundles of blankets.

"Look what Papa has," said Mama.

Grandma pulled away the blankets, and there were two more babies!

"You got three babies!" said Bernard.

"They're triplets," said Mama.

"What's that one?"

"That is Baby Sadie," said Papa.

"And this is Baby Sue," said Grandma.

"Now you have two sisters and a brother."

"Isn't it wonderful?" said Mama.

"I only wanted one baby," said Bernard.

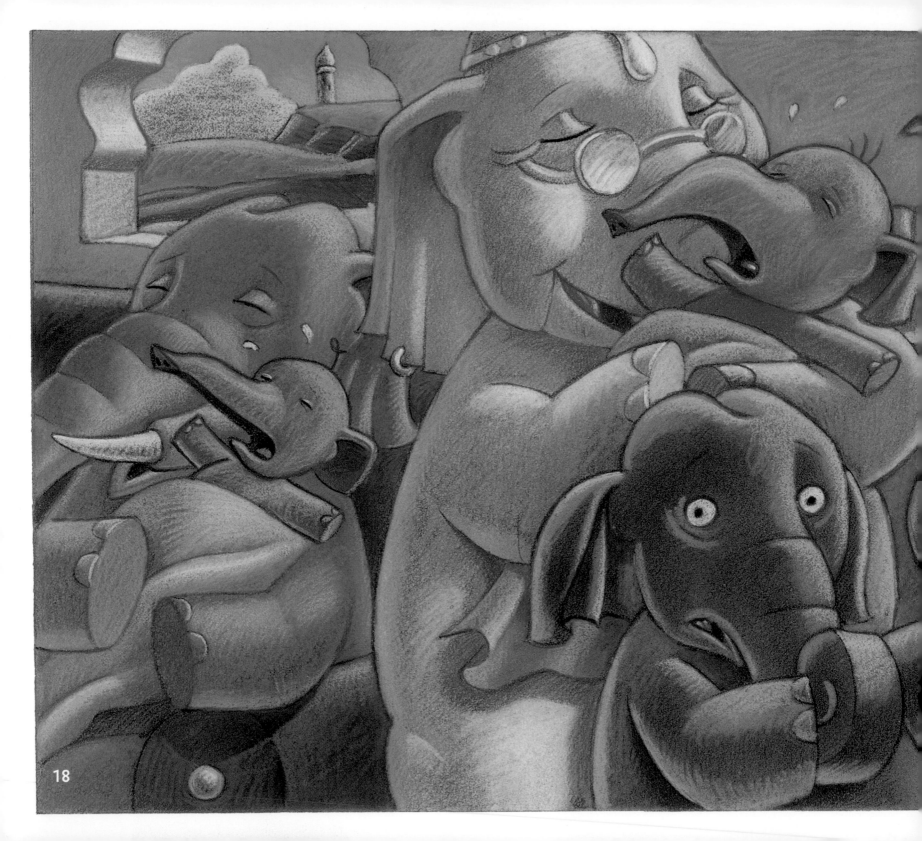

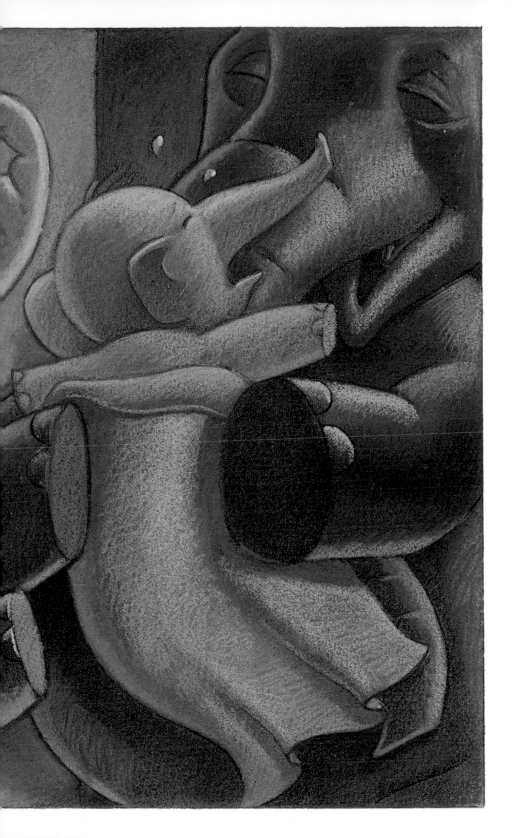

Pretty soon all three babies began to cry.

"I didn't want a crying baby," said Bernard.

"All babies cry," said Mama.

"That's how they tell us what they need," said Grandma.

"They need to be quiet," said Bernard.

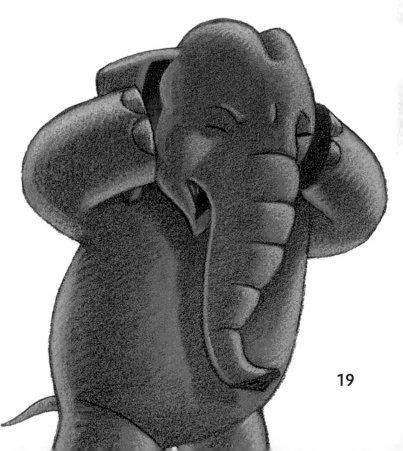

19

When Sue slept, Max cried.

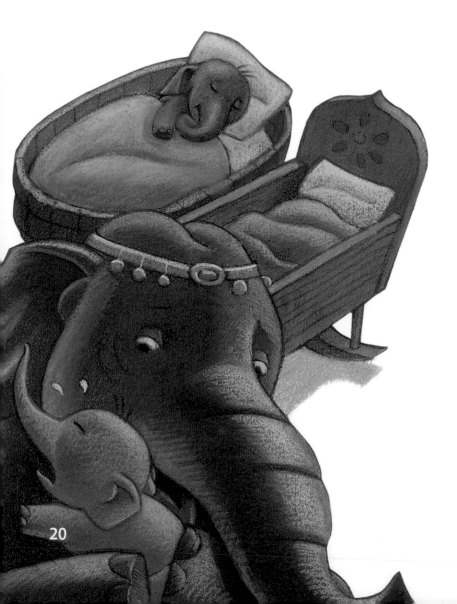

When Max slept, Sadie cried.

When Sadie slept, both Max and Sue cried.
Sue spit up, too.
"Take her back," said Bernard.
"All babies spit up," said Papa.
Sure enough, Max and Sadie spit up.

When they weren't crying or spitting up, they made pee-pee and poop.

"Stinky," said Bernard.

No one else seemed to mind.

"Aren't they adorable," said Grandma.

"So sweet," said Mama.

"Our little babies," said Papa.

"Yuck," said Bernard. He went to his room and slammed the door.

Pretty soon Mama, Papa, and Grandma came, carrying the triplets, and sat on the bed with Bernard.

"What's the matter?" asked Mama.

"This is not what I wanted," said Bernard.

"What?" Papa asked.

"I just wanted one baby brother, who wouldn't spit up, cry, poop, and take up all the room in Mama's lap," said Bernard.

"Three babies are more than we expected," said Papa.

"They do take up a lot of time," said Grandma.

"But we will always have time for you," said Papa.

"And there will always be room for you on my lap," said Mama.

She handed Sue to Grandma, and hugged Bernard.

Bernard sighed and leaned back against Mama.

Sue, Sadie, and Max snoozed peacefully. They each had wispy hair, floppy pink ears, and little curled-up trunks.

"They're cute when they sleep," said Bernard.

"Soon they'll be cute all the time," said Grandma.

"Just like you," said Mama.

"Can you wait till then?" asked Papa.
"Oh, all right," said Bernard.